Alexander, Who Used to Be Rich Last Sunday

JUDITH VIORST

Illustrated by RAY CRUZ

Atheneum Books for Young Readers
New York London Toronto Sydney New Delhi

Atheneum Books for Young Readers
An imprint of Simon & Schuster
Children's Publishing Division
1230 Avenue of the Americas
New York, NY 10020
Text copyright © 1978 by Judith Viorst
Illustrations copyright © 1978 by Ray Cruz
All rights reserved including the right of reproduction
in whole or in part in any form.
First Aladdin Paperbacks edition, 1980
Second Aladdin Paperbacks edition, 1988
Also available in a hardcover edition from Atheneum Books for Young Readers
Manufactured in China

60 59 58 57 56 55 54 53 52 51

Library of Congress Cataloging-in-Publication Data
Viorst, Judith.
   Alexander, who used to be rich last Sunday.
   Reprint. Originally published: New York:
Atheneum, 1978.
   Summary: Although Alexander and his money are
quickly parted, he comes to realize all the things
that can be done with a dollar.
   [1. Finance, Personal—Fiction.   2. Humorous stories]
I. Cruz, Ray, ill.   II. Title.
[PZ7.V816Am 1988]   [E]   87-14330
ISBN: 978-0-689-71199-2 (pbk.)
ISBN: 978-1-4424-6317-2 (eBook)

0314 SCP

To the boys' Grandma Betty and Grandpa Louie Viorst

It isn't fair that my brother Anthony has two dollars and three quarters and one dime and seven nickels and eighteen pennies.

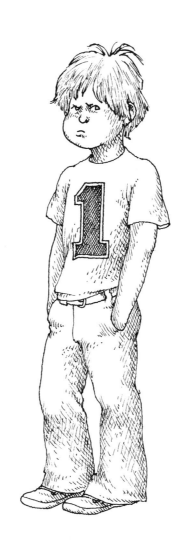

It isn't fair that my brother Nicholas has one dollar and two quarters and five dimes and five nickels and thirteen pennies.

It isn't fair because what I've got is...bus tokens.

And most of the time what I've mostly got is...bus tokens.

And even when I'm very rich, I know that pretty soon what I'll have is...bus tokens.

I know because I used to be rich. Last Sunday.

Last Sunday Grandma Betty and Grandpa Louie came to visit from New Jersey.
They brought lox because my father likes to eat lox. They brought
plants because my mother likes to grow plants.

They brought a dollar for me and a dollar for Nick and a dollar for Anthony because—Mom says it isn't nice to say this—we like money.

A lot. Especially me.

My father told me to put the dollar away to pay for college.

He was kidding.

Anthony told me to use the dollar to go downtown to a store and buy a new face. Anthony stinks.

Nicky said to take the dollar and bury it in the garden and in a week a dollar tree would grow. Ha ha ha.

Mom said if I really want to buy a walkie-talkie, save my money.

Saving money is hard.

Because last Sunday, when I used to be rich, I went to Pearson's Drug Store and got bubble gum. And after the gum stopped tasting good, I got more gum. And after that gum stopped tasting good, I got more gum. And even though I told my friend David I'd sell him all the gum in my mouth for a nickel, he still wouldn't buy it.

Good-bye fifteen cents.

Last Sunday, when I used to be rich, I bet that I could hold my breath till 300. Anthony won. I bet that I could jump from the top of the stoop and land on my feet. Nicky won.

I bet that I could hide this purple marble in my hand,
and my mom would never guess which hand I was hiding it in.
I didn't know that moms made children pay.

Good-bye another fifteen cents.

I absolutely was saving the rest of my money. I positively was saving the rest of my money. Except that Eddie called me up and said that he would rent me his snake for an hour. I always wanted to rent his snake for an hour.

Good-bye twelve cents.

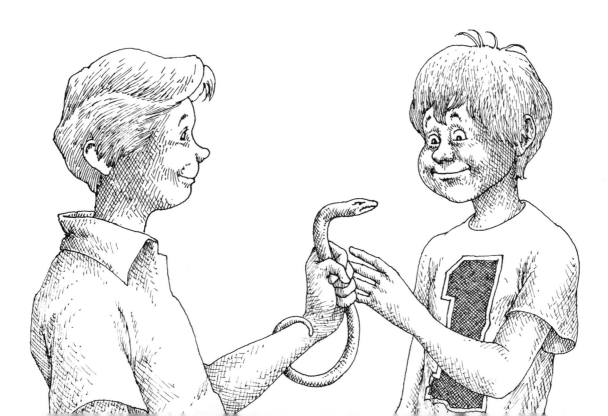

Anthony said when I'm ninety-nine I still won't have enough for a walkie-talkie. Nick said I'm too dumb to be let loose. My father said that there are certain words a boy can never say, no matter how ratty and mean his brothers are being. My father fined me five cents each for saying them.

Good-bye dime.

Last Sunday, when I used to be rich, by accident I flushed three cents down the toilet. A nickel fell through a crack when I walked on my hands. I tried to get my nickel out with a butter knife and also my mother's scissors.

Good-bye eight cents.

And the butter knife.

And the scissors.

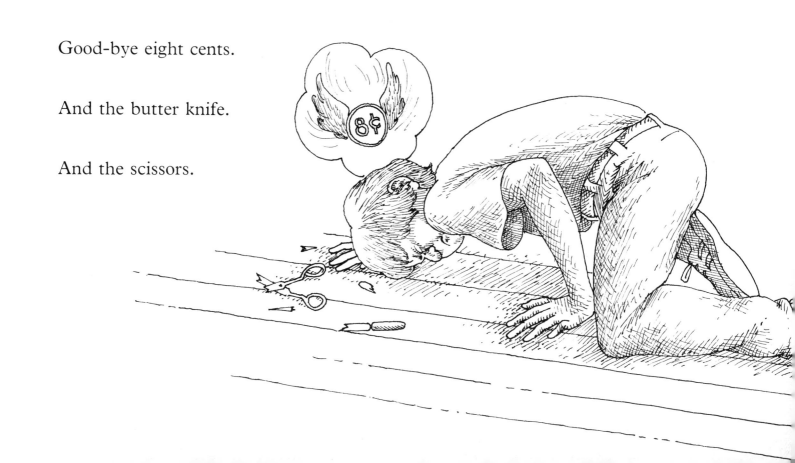

Last Sunday, when I used to be rich, I found this chocolate candy bar just sitting there. I rescued it from being melted or smushed. Except the way I rescued it from being melted or smushed was that I ate it. How was I supposed to know it was Anthony's?

Good-bye eleven cents.

I absolutely was saving the rest of my money. I positively was saving the rest of my money. But then Nick did a magic trick that made my pennies vanish in thin air. The trick to bring them back he hasn't learned yet.

Good-bye four cents.

Anthony said that even when I'm 199, I still won't have enough for
a walkie-talkie. Nick said they should lock me in a cage. My father
said that there are certain things a boy can never kick, no matter how
ratty and mean his brothers are being. My father made me pay five cents
for kicking it.

Good-bye nickel.

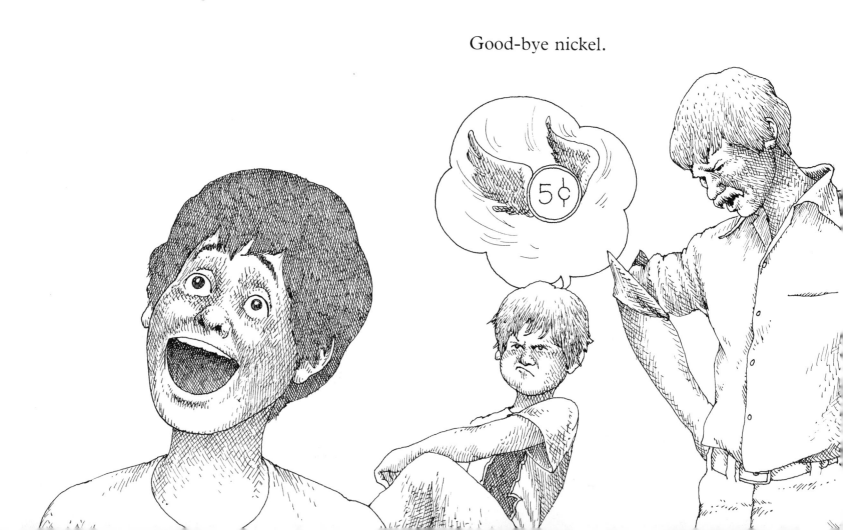

Last Sunday, when I used to be rich, Cathy around the corner had a garage sale. I positively only went to look. I looked at a half-melted candle. I needed that candle. I looked at a bear with one eye. I needed that bear. I looked at a deck of cards that was perfect except for no seven of clubs and no two of diamonds. I didn't need that seven or that two.

Good-bye twenty cents.

I absolutely was saving the rest of my money. I positively was saving the rest of my money. I absolutely positively was saving the rest of my money. Except I needed to get some money to save.

I tried to make a tooth fall out—I could put it under my pillow and get a quarter. No loose teeth.

I looked in Pearson's telephone booths for nickels and dimes that people sometimes forget. No one forgot.

I brought some non-returnable bottles down to Friendly's Market.
Friendly's Market wasn't very friendly.

I told my grandma and grandpa to come back soon.

Last Sunday, when I used to be rich, I used to have a dollar. I do not have a dollar any more. I've got this dopey deck of cards. I've got this one-eyed bear. I've got this melted candle.

And...some bus tokens.

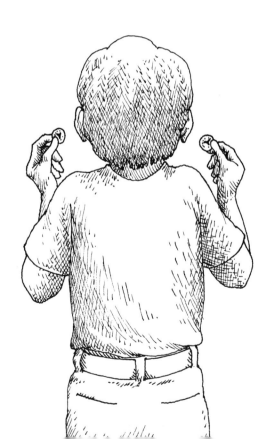